The Unruly Robin

The Unruly

by DORATHEA

Dorathea Dankooszk

Robin

DANA, *pseud.* ILLUSTRATIONS BY THE AUTHOR

Dankovszky

ABELARD PRESS NEW YORK

jII231u

BOOKS BY DORATHEA DANA
The Unruly Robin
Sugar Bush
Casey Joins the Circus

Lithographed in the United States of America.
Published simultaneously in Canada by Nelson, Foster & Scott, Ltd.

FOR

SUE
KIP
& RICKY

JIMMY
&
JOEY

DONNIE
& BONNIE

JACKIE &
JEFF

Dean and Delia Davis knelt on the sunroom sofa, their noses pressed flat against the cold win-

dowpane. The twins were watching a spring storm. They tried to see how far they could count between each flash of lightning and the boom of thunder which followed.

Weejee, their half-grown kitten, stood on his hind legs between them, trying to catch the raindrops that danced across the outside of the pane.

Zing!

7

Again, a blinding zigzag of light leaped through the billowing black clouds.

"One, two, three, four," counted Dean, as they waited for the thunder. "It's getting farther away."

Then it came! Crash! Bang! The windows rattled and shook, as the echo rumbled far off over the hills.

Delia turned and sniffed the air. "I smell the cookies," she said. "They're just beginning to brown."

On rainy days, the children's mother always baked. It helped to take the dampness out of the air, she said. Sometimes, even on a sunny day, when the twins thought of the butter cookies she made, they wished that it would rain because then they would all work together in the kitchen, as they had today.

After Mrs. Davis rolled the dough flat, Dean and Delia cut out the cookies. They used their animal cookie-cutters, and poked a raisin into the dough for each animal's eye. The first ones were

8

samples, just baked for tasting, and now the twins could hardly wait until they were done.

Another flash of lightning made them turn back to the window. Dean counted all the way to ten before the thunder sounded, this time far away. Then they heard their mother coming through the living room.

"The cookies must be done." Delia jumped down from the sofa with Dean and Weejee after her.

"The storm is almost over, children," Mrs. Davis said, as she placed a plate of cookies on the sun-room table. "Here are your tasters, one for each of you. Be careful, they're hot."

"A squirrel cookie, a rabbit cookie, and a bird cookie." Dean looked them over.

"I'll take the squirrel," said Delia. "He's the one I put an extra ear on."

"I'll take the rabbit," Dean decided. "I gave him two eyes."

"And that leaves the bird for Weejee," said Mrs.

Davis, as she put the cookie down on a newspaper for the kitten.

Weejee was still too young to know that cats are not supposed to like cookies, particularly hot ones. He bit into it and jumped straight up into the air. Then he hissed. He reached out his paw and touched it carefully, pushing it around on the paper until it had cooled off. Mrs. Davis and the children laughed.

"I hope that's the only kind of bird he ever

eats," Delia said. "I think kittens are more fun than anything."

The room suddenly brightened as the sun came from behind a dark cloud.

"The rain is over, the rain is over," the twins sang. "Mother, may we go out?"

"Put on your rubbers and sweaters, and try to keep out of the mud." As she spoke, Mrs. Davis opened the door to let in the lovely fresh smell of the spring rain.

Out to the garden the twins ran, to see what had happened to the seeds they had planted not so long ago. Between each row flowed rivers of rain water, and seeds floated everywhere. The little tomato plants were flat on their faces in the mud.

"It's a good thing we have some seeds left," Delia said sadly, "because now we have to plant another garden."

"Just think of all the funny places those seeds will grow," said Dean. "They're floating around

11

in Mother's flowers now. She won't know whether they are radishes or petunias or what. Look at Weejee!" he cried suddenly.

The kitten tore out of the grass into the garden, slid to a stop, and began sinking into the wet earth. He lifted each paw and shook it, spreading his toes as wide apart as he could, but still he sank down. He looked so funny up to his knees in mud, that the children laughed, but they went at once to help him. Delia picked him up and carried him to the grass.

Weejee did not look like a cat at all, with his fur flat and wet, and his feet blobs of mud. He looked more like Donald Duck. Mrs. Davis shook her head at them from the window. Then she went to find some rags to wipe up the mud she knew they would bring in with them.

"Weejee is pretending he's a tiger in the jungle," said Dean, as the kitten slipped out of Delia's hands and began to squirm through the grass on his stomach.

"He's just wiping off the mud," Delia answered. "Look! He's found something."

Weejee put out his paw and carefully touched a small object. He crept closer and sniffed. He sat down beside it, wet but pleased.

"What can it be?" Dean asked, as they tiptoed closer.

With his head on one side, the kitten tapped his find gently. He bent his head to the other side, and tapped the thing again with his opposite paw. Then he saw the children. He picked up the small pale something in his mouth and trotted to the kitchen door, his short wet tail straight with pride.

"Look, Mother!" Dean called. "Weejee has something in his mouth."

Mrs. Davis held the door open and the kitten marched in. The twins followed him. When he got to the exact middle of the kitchen, he laid his prize on the floor and sat down, waiting for praise.

"Why, Weejee!" Delia exclaimed, patting his

damp head. "Whatever did you find? What is it?"

"It's a dead baby bird, just out of the shell," answered Mrs. Davis. "It looks like a robin to me. It's too young to have any feathers. Probably the storm blew it out of its nest."

"Now we'll have to bury it." Dean held it up by one thread of a claw. "We can put it in a matchbox and have a funeral."

"Wait, children," said their mother. "We must first be sure that it's dead."

She poured hot water into a cup and spread an old handkerchief over it. On this she laid the tiny, still bird. Steam came up all around him.

"Let's see," she went on, taking down a bottle of vanilla extract from the shelf. "I think this may be strong enough to do him some good."

She opened the queer-looking triangle of a mouth and gently poured a drop of vanilla down the throat.

The children were breathless. They watched and watched, but nothing happened.

14

The kitten sat on the window sill, watching too.

"Look at that wet cat!" exclaimed Mrs. Davis, snatching him down. "Oh, my clean curtains! Delia, get Weejee's towel and dry his fur."

While Delia was rubbing the kitten dry, Dean was allowed to stack the cookies in the cookie jar.

"That robin bird looks like this cookie," Dean said, holding up a bird cookie with a big black raisin eye. "They're both bare."

"He won't look like a real bird until he grows some feathers," Mrs. Davis answered. "And Dean, don't look so fondly at that cookie. No more for a while."

As she spoke, she glanced over at the little bird. Could she believe her eyes, or had he really moved? She did not want to raise the children's hopes too soon, so she went over quietly and picked him up in the handkerchief. He twitched the tiniest bit. There was no doubt about it. He was still alive.

16

Mrs. Davis sighed. She was glad, but she was sorry too. She thought of the long weeks of trouble ahead, as the children raised another little pet by hand. It seemed they were always bringing something home to be taken care of. She wondered what their father would say. He certainly would not be pleased.

The twins were watching her.

"Is he alive?" they asked in one breath.

"Just barely," she answered. "We mustn't handle

him. Dean, get some cotton from the bathroom cabinet. We'll make a soft nest for him in the matchbox you have, and put him in a warm place until he gets stronger."

Later in the afternoon, when the children were drinking their cold milk and eating their cookies, they made plans for bringing up the baby robin.

"But birds don't drink milk," Delia said. "Mother, what do baby birds eat?"

"Just what grown-up birds eat," Mrs. Davis answered. "Lots of nice juicy worms."

"We can get him some when we plant the rest of the seeds tomorrow," Dean planned. "How long till Daddy comes home, Mother? I can hardly wait to tell him about the bird."

Mrs. Davis looked at the kitchen clock. "Just a little over an hour. I must put the potatoes in the oven."

Dean and Delia walked to the corner to meet their father. Weejee scampered along beside them.

When Mr. Davis stepped off the bus, the twins ran to him and each one took a hand. Both talked at once, and by the time they arrived at the gate Mr. Davis knew all about the baby bird.

Mrs. Davis was waiting for them. She opened the gate and took her husband's arm, shooing the twins ahead of her. Together the family went into the kitchen and looked at the little bird lying in his cotton nest. Weejee climbed on to Mr. Davis' shoulder to look. The robin seemed as dead as ever.

19

"So we've done it again," said Mr. Davis, shaking his head sadly. "The Davis Rescue Mission. When business is slow our trained cat, Weejee, goes out and picks up customers."

He pulled the kitten down and set him on the floor with a pat. Then he picked up the matchbox nest and looked at the bird closely. The scrawny heap of skin and bones unfolded itself, the head lifted a little, and the mouth opened silently.

"Aha!" cried Mr. Davis. "He salutes the hand that will feed him."

"We're in for it, I guess," sighed Mrs. Davis. "I hope you feel strong enough to go out and spade up the garden again after dinner. The storm washed most of the children's seeds out of the ground."

"And we have to find worms for the robin's breakfast," Delia added.

"Now it begins," said her father. "Why can't he eat bread crumbs?"

"Well, his mother feeds him worms," Dean

told him, "and she must know what's best for him. Don't you think so, Daddy?"

"Best for him, perhaps," Mr. Davis answered, "but what about us? It keeps a pair of robins busy from dawn till dark finding food for their babies, and they know where to look."

"But they have three or four to feed," said Delia, "and we have only one. Besides, he couldn't possibly eat very much, he's so little."

"What we really should do," Mr. Davis said, "is to train Weejee for the job. After all, it's his robin."

They all laughed and looked at the kitten. He lay on his back under the table, pulling on the cloth with his front paws, and kicking it madly with his back ones.

"Stop it!" Mrs. Davis cried, swooping to pick him up.

Like a spring, the little cat snapped into the air, landing stiff-legged on all fours. With his head held to one side, and his tail as bushy as a squirrel's, he bounced around the dining room like a mechanical toy.

"He's a clown." Mrs. Davis smiled in spite of herself as she smoothed out the crumpled corner of the tablecloth.

Shortly after supper, the children and their father went out in the garden and for a while worked hard. Mr. Davis straightened the little tomato plants by piling mud around them, and the twins dug for worms. But the ground was still too wet, and Mr. Davis decided to wait until it dried a little to plant more seeds.

"How did you make out with the worms?" he asked the twins. "Did you find any?"

"We have three," Dean answered proudly. "One for breakfast, one for lunch, and one for supper."

"He'll want them all for breakfast," said their father. But even he did not know much about a robin's appetite.

Mrs. Davis met them at the door.

"I hope you had some luck," she said, "because the little bird is hungry."

"Then we can feed him now," the twins cried.

Mrs. Davis held the bird in her hand, and Dean dangled a worm in front of him. The robin lay there, as if asleep. Gently Delia pried open his bill and Dean dropped in the end of the worm.

In a flash the robin came to life. He opened his mouth wider, stretched his neck, swallowed. Presto! The worm was gone.

It happened so fast they could not believe their eyes. There the bird lay in Mrs. Davis' hand, as dead-looking as ever.

They tried it again. They opened his beak, and as soon as the robin felt the end of the worm in his throat he came to life and swallowed it. The next second he collapsed into a lifeless heap of skin and bones.

"Why, it's magical!" exclaimed Mr. Davis. "I wonder what a cup of coffee would do to him?"

"Shall I give him the last one?" Dean asked. "He must still be hungry."

"Yes, give it to him," said his mother, holding the bird's beak open. Gulp! The worm was gone.

"Now what have you got for his breakfast?" their father wanted to know. "You'll have to get up earlier than the Early Bird if you want to find worms."

"Goodness!" exclaimed Mrs. Davis, glancing at the clock. "To bed with all of you—children, bird and cat. To bed!"

Dean and Delia were almost asleep when they heard a queer noise, a high thin *squawk, squawk!*

"What's that, do you suppose?" whispered Delia, raising herself on her elbow to listen.

"It sounds like a chicken with its head caught in a door," Dean answered, "but no one around here keeps chickens."

"It's much farther away now, isn't it?" Delia said sleepily.

"Now it's almost gone." And she forgot to listen any more as she drifted off to sleep.

But Dean was still listening. He heard the back door open, footsteps on the lawn, and a low muttering. Then he saw the reflection of a flashlight on the ceiling. He jumped out of bed and ran over to the window.

There was his father, flashlight in hand, walking slowly through the grass, talking to himself. Dean looked around, but Delia was sound asleep.

"Daddy," he called in a low voice through the screen, "what are you doing?"

Mr. Davis was so busy he hardly bothered to look up.

"Go back to bed," he said. "I'm trying to find some night crawlers so your new pet won't keep the whole neighborhood awake all night. Didn't you hear him?"

"Yes, we did. What are night crawlers, Daddy?"

"Worms, Dean, large lively worms, which only come out at night. Now get back to bed this minute."

In the morning, when the children ran to see the bird, he was very much alive. He looked fatter, they thought.

CHAPTER 3

"No wonder," said their mother, "with the huge night crawlers your father caught, and had to cut up to feed him to keep him quiet."

"So that's the noise we heard!" exclaimed Delia. "Why didn't you wake me up, Dean? We could have gone out and helped Daddy."

"You may spend all your time after school at

worm-collecting," their mother told them, "so your poor father won't have to do it again tonight."

As soon as the twins got home from school, they ran out in the garden and began to dig. They dug and they dug. Finally, they found a worm.

"Only one little thin worm," sighed Delia. "We'll never find enough."

"Well, maybe this isn't good worm ground," suggested Dean. "Let's go farther down the street."

"Come on, Weejee," Delia called, as they started off. "You've got to help us."

The spring air was as cool and sweet against their cheeks as a bunch of violets from the woods. The tiny new leaves on the maple trees made a thin shade on the ground beneath.

"The shade from the trees comes out in the spring just like the leaves," said Delia. "It grows deeper and deeper as the leaves grow bigger and bigger."

"Look!" cried Dean. "There's old Ben, digging a garden for Mrs. Moore. Let's ask for some worms."

They climbed up a grassy bank to the white picket fence.

"Hello, Ben," Dean called. "Are there any worms in this garden?"

"You goin' a-fish?" asked the old man, coming over to the fence. He was the Italian handyman of the neighborhood, and next to making gardens, he liked to fish.

"No, we have a baby bird and he has to have worms to eat, lots of them," Delia told him, holding up the tin can. "Our garden hasn't got very many, and we thought maybe ·we could have some of yours."

"Sure, sure," chuckled old Ben. "I getta worms, plenty worms. You come back after a while."

He put his foot on the shovel and turned over a big piece of moist chocolate-colored earth. Then he bent down and pulled out a long unwilling worm.

"See?" He dropped it into the tin can. "Ben finda plenty worms." Then he found a few more.

The children skipped happily home. Weejee
ran after them.

"It's all fixed, Mother," Delia called, as they
banged noisily into the kitchen.

"Old Ben is digging worms for us," Dean said.

30

"That's very kind of him, I'm sure," said Mrs. Davis, "but I know that Mrs. Moore is paying him to spade up her garden, not to find worms for a bird. You children will have to do that for yourselves."

"Pete—Pete—Pete!" shrieked the little bird, rocking back on his heels with each blast.

"How can he make so much noise?" Delia marveled. "He's so little."

"We can call him Pete," said Dean, "and we can feed him right now."

As soon as old Ben's worms were gone, Pete began all over again. Mrs. Davis and the children could hardly endure it.

"I'm sure your father won't put up with this," their mother said.

Dean took the empty can and went back to old Ben to get more worms.

"What can we do?" Delia asked her mother. "Can we try to get the parent birds to take him back?"

"Why, yes, we might try that," Mrs. Davis

agreed. "We can put him out on the lawn just about where Weejee found him."

"Look!" cried Dean, as he came in a little later, tin can held high. "It's almost full."

"Hurray! Now we can give him all he can eat. Let's start." And Delia began to feed Pete. "One, two, three, four, five, six, seven," she counted. "How many worms *could* he eat?"

"That's enough," Dean said. "We've got to make these last." He looked worriedly into the can.

"Now let's put him out on the lawn and see whether his parents will find him," Delia announced. "This was just about the place, wasn't it, Mother?" she called a few minutes later.

"Yes," her mother answered. "Now leave him there, children, and come in, so you won't frighten the old birds."

They watched a while from the back porch, but there were no birds around anywhere. Then they forgot to watch.

"Pete—Pete—Pete—Pete!" The raw shrill sound cut through the spring afternoon.

Delia heard it. At first she could not think what it was. Then she realized it was the bird! He 'must still be out on the lawn. Maybe his parents had found him. She ran to the window.

There was the robin, making as much noise as he could. Near him sat Weejee, but Weejee was watching something else. It was old Pegleg the Pirate, a battle-scarred tomcat from the next block.

33

"Dean! Dean!" Delia screamed, as she ran downstairs. "Help me save the robin!"

Out the front door she ran, to the rescue. She picked up the robin and Dean ran after her, chasing old Pegleg. Out of the bushes ran Tiger, the gray striped cat from next door.

"Well, if one hadn't gotten him, the other one would have," Mrs. Davis said, when they brought the bird back on the porch. "We might have known this would happen. This is a cat neighborhood, and that noise would attract them all. Dean, give him a few worms to keep him quiet."

A few worms every few minutes was what the bird wanted. If he did not get them, he sat back on his heels and shrieked, "Pete—Pete—Pete!"

"Anyway, Pete's a good name for him," Delia remarked. "That's all he ever says."

Three more times before Mr. Davis came home, they had to feed the robin. The worms were half-gone.

34

"We'll have to find a lot more for him tomorrow," said Dean, looking into the can. "I wonder where we'd better go?"

"So your first day as foster parents to a robin has kept you stepping," their father laughed, when he heard all about it that night. "But I think old Ben took most of the load off your shoulders."

"It's funny Pete has been quiet for so long," said Delia, tiptoeing out to look at him.

The bird heard her. He raised his head and began, "Pete—Pete—Pete!"

"What a racket!" exclaimed Mr. Davis. "He's twice as loud since last night. And why have you named him Pete?"

"Because that's what he says," Dean explained.

"Children, children!" Mr. Davis shook his head sadly. "How can you have made such a mistake?"

"Why, Daddy," Delia said, "just listen to him. It's as plain as anything. Pete, Pete, Pete!"

"And what does he mean?"

"He means he's hungry and wants to eat," Dean insisted.

"That's what he's saying—Eat, eat, eat." Their father was firm.

Mrs. Davis laughed. "You're right," she said. "It *is* very plain."

"It sounds like *eat* to me, too, Daddy," Delia agreed.

"It still sounds like *Pete* to me," Dean said, listening.

"The big thing is to keep him quiet and well-behaved," Mr. Davis told them. "He's an unruly robin."

"This is the thirty-second worm today," Delia complained, as she fed Pete. "Of course, some of them weren't very big."

"Now I see why it is there aren't so many bugs where there are lots of birds," Mr. Davis remarked. "Birds eat as many bugs as they do worms. I hope Pete works in our garden when he grows up."

That evening, when they were out in the garden
again, there were hardly any worms to be found.
But the next day was Saturday, and the twins went
up and down their own street, and around the
block. Wherever anyone was working in a garden,
Dean and Delia stopped and asked for worms. They
managed to collect quite a few.

On Sunday they were lucky, too, because their
father helped them. He found a nice, wet, wormy-
looking place down beside the brook. Sure enough,
they almost filled the can.

"Now we're a little ahead," Delia sighed happily.
"But how will we keep them until we need them?"

"In the refrigerator, of course," her father replied.

"Oh, Mother will never let us." And Delia shook her head.

"Why won't she?" Mr. Davis inquired.

"She just won't," said Dean. "I know."

"What's in that can?" Mrs. Davis asked a few minutes later, as her husband opened the refrigerator door.

"Worms, dear," her husband said casually. "Pete's food for the next forty-eight hours."

"Worms in the refrigerator!" she cried. "Whatever are you thinking of?"

"Nice clean worms in a nice clean can," Mr. Davis said reasonably. "Where else would we keep them?"

"Anywhere else," said Mrs. Davis firmly, standing in front of the icebox door. "Anywhere else at all."

"Now, dear," coaxed her husband, "chickens eat worms, and you keep chickens in the refrigerator. We just ate one for dinner," he added brightly. "A chicken, I mean."

"That has nothing to do with it. I will not have worms in the refrigerator."

Mr. Davis knew Mrs. Davis quite well. He turned to the children. "Your mother won't have the worms in the refrigerator. Have you any other suggestions?"

The twins were laughing. "We knew she wouldn't," Delia giggled.

"We can keep them down by the brook," Dean suggested.

"Fine," agreed his father. "That's cool enough for them."

Every day Pete grew fatter, and a few more downy feathers sprouted. Every day his appetite was bigger and the worm supply smaller. His squawks sounded as if they came out of a radio that was turned on full blast.

The only time the robin was quiet was when he slept. He lived in a market basket set on an old table on the screened-in porch. He had learned to climb up on the rim, and from here he ruled the household. A fat ball of down, he

41

rocked himself back and forth with his demands for more and bigger worms.

The milkman tiptoed up the back steps before dawn, and tried not to rattle the bottles. He knew what happened when he woke Pete. Mr. Davis stole out to the kitchen in his stockinged feet for his midnight snack, but Pete's quick ears always heard him, and the din began:

"Eat! Eat! Eat!"

The children were worn out collecting worms, and the neighbors were worn out helping them.

"There just aren't any more worms left around here," Delia said sadly.

"Besides, everyone's garden is all planted now," Dean added. "We never see anyone digging any more."

"This is a fine state of affairs," their father declared. "For blocks around people turn away when they see us coming. Something has to be done. Our friends have been wormed away from us."

"Well, I've been giving him scraped beef rolled into little balls," said Mrs. Davis, "but he still prefers worms."

"There just aren't any more," Delia said again. "We've looked and looked."

"I wish we knew where old Ben is working now." Dean looked thoughtful. "Remember all the worms he gave us? There were so many in the can, he said they looked like spaghetti."

"Spaghetti." Mr. Davis repeated the word slowly. "I wonder."

"What, Daddy?" asked the twins.

"We can try it. We've *got* to try it."

"What is it?" teased the children. "Tell us."

"Spaghetti," said Mr. Davis. "Perhaps we can fool Pete with it."

"We could dangle it just like worms." Dean laughed at the thought of it.

"But it wouldn't taste just like worms," objected Delia. She did not think it was funny.

"Now really, Delia," her father said. "How do you know what a worm tastes like?"

"That has nothing to do with it, I'm sure," Mrs. Davis agreed with her husband. "It's only the shape that counts. We'll try it. We'll have spaghetti for supper, and only hope that Pete likes it too."

"Our future hangs by a thread," Mr. Davis whispered, "a thread of spaghetti. But for Pete's sake, have supper early. He's starving."

44

"If he doesn't like spaghetti, what *shall* we give him?" Mrs. Davis asked.

"We'll give him away," her husband replied.

"You're mistaken, dear. I've already tried."

"Oh, Mother!" Delia wailed. "You've tried to give him away?"

"I certainly have," she said, "but no one would take him."

As soon as the spaghetti was cooked, Mrs. Davis held up a few strands on a fork to cool. The family stood around breathlessly, waiting for the test. Weejee watched, too, his whiskers at an excited angle. He climbed up on a chair and batted at the spaghetti. One long strand fell down and wrapped itself around the cat's head. He backed all around the kitchen trying to get away from it.

Pete clutched the rim of his basket, as he wobbled back and forth squawking, "Eat—eat—eat!"

"Now cut it into worm lengths," Mr. Davis directed, "and we're ready."

He dangled an end down Pete's open gullet. Gulp! It disappeared. Another and another spaghetti worm followed.

Mrs. Davis sighed with relief. "Try some of the meatballs, too," she suggested, "so his diet won't be too one-sided."

Pete swallowed the morsel of meat, and batted his eyes around contentedly. He settled his big funny mouth down on his chest, wobbled a few more times, and went to sleep.

"Success!" announced Mr. Davis. "Spaghetti and meatballs. I guess Pete must be part Italian."

"Hurray!" shouted Dean and Delia, as they joined hands and danced around the porch.

"Now we can play again," Dean said joyfully. "We don't have to look for any more worms."

"Peace, blessed peace," Mr. Davis said. "Why didn't we think of this before?"

So Pete had spaghetti as often as he got hungry, and he loved it.

Soon Pete began to look more like a bird. He was downy and speckled, and his wings had strong little feathers at the tips. He often stretched them for exercise. Finally, he climbed up on the handle of the basket and used his wings to help himself.

"He's ready to fly," Mrs. Davis said.

"He should have been flying long ago," Mr. Davis remarked.

"Why doesn't he try?" asked Delia.

"He has to have someone to teach him," Dean

answered. "But how can we do it, when we don't know how ourselves?"

"That's silly," Delia said. "We'll just push him off things till he learns."

So that afternoon they put a pillow on the floor and pushed Pete off the table. Plunk! He fell like a bag of beans.

"It's a good thing we had the pillow there," Delia said. "Let's try it again."

Pete did not like it. He squawked loudly.

"What's the matter with the bird?" Mrs. Davis called.

"We're teaching him to fly," the twins replied.

"Take him outdoors where there's more room," their mother suggested. "But let's wait till Daddy comes home."

That evening Mr. Davis did everything he could think of. He swung Pete gently to and fro in his hands. Then he let him go. Pete just squawked, and the next time held on harder.

"And I thought it was born in a bird to know how to fly, just like a fish swims," Mr. Davis said.

"He can't learn all at once," Delia answered sympathetically. "Let's wait until tomorrow for another lesson."

"In the meantime, hang his basket in a tree," their father directed, "and he may get some pointers from the other birds."

"But watch the cats," Mrs. Davis cautioned. "They can climb right up there."

"Oh, Weejee will fight them off, won't you, Weejee?" And Dean put the kitten in the robin's basket.

The next evening and the next, Pete had a lesson in how to fly. A breeze was blowing, and Mr. Davis tossed him gently into it. His wings spread, Pete glided to the grass.

"Now he's getting the idea," Dean cried. "Do it again, Daddy, before he forgets."

Mr. Davis tossed him a little higher up into the air. Down he came, right on Mr. Davis' head.

"A tree has nothing on me," he observed, trying to get hold of Pete. "I, too, have robins in my hair." They took him up on the porch. "Now let's give him a longer ride."

This time Pete landed on Dean's head.

Then they took him to the window on the stair landing. He side-slipped a little as he came down, so that he could land on Mr. Davis' head again. No matter how they ran from him, it seemed he could always stay in the air long enough to catch one of them. When he got down too low, of course, he had to land on the grass. But he soon found a remedy for that—he landed on Weejee's head.

The first time it happened the kitten was flattened out on the grass in surprise. He shook the robin off and stood looking at him. Then he sat down sadly and never took his eyes off him again. When he saw Pete coming for him, he tried to duck, but he was often caught. He just stood patiently until someone picked the bird off his head.

Suddenly, on one toss, the little bird began beating the air with his wings.

"Look! Look!" shouted the twins. "He's flying!"

After that, each time Pete was thrown into the air, he flew a little.

"Now if we can just teach him to feed himself," Mr. Davis said, "we shall have won our freedom."

"He's learning," Delia told him. "We put bugs in front of him and he puts his bill down beside them, but he just doesn't know enough to pick them up."

"He just opens his mouth and expects the bugs to walk in," Dean said. "He's pretty dumb."

Once Pete landed on a branch of a tree. After wobbling around a while, he flew to a higher branch and then to a still higher one, out of sight.

"Pete's gone!" Delia wailed. "Here, Pete! Here, Pete!"

Out of the tree he came, pumping away for dear life. Plunk!

"Why, he comes when he's called!" Dean exclaimed. "Now we needn't be afraid he'll fly away."

The next day Pete stayed up in the tree. He came whenever he was called, landing on the children's heads, but he went right back to the tree. That evening, when the family was in the garden, he flew to the roof of the house, and sat there watching them. Dean found a bug and called him.

Back of a hydrangea bush, out of sight, sat old Pegleg the Pirate. He was just waiting. Down came

Pete like a bag of sand, on top of the cat's head.

"Yeeeeeeee-ow!" shrieked the Pirate. He raced across the garden, tumbling Pete into the spinach.

"Save him! Save him!" screamed Delia.

"Save which?" her father asked. "Poor old Pegleg is probably out in the lot having a heart attack right now."

"The next time it won't be so funny," Mrs. Davis told them. "Every day those cats prowl around here, waiting for a chance at Pete."

"And he thinks all cats are friendly, like Weejee," Delia said. "We can't leave him out here alone. He'll land on them whenever he sees them. What shall we do?"

"I was afraid this would happen," their mother said. "You know this is a cat neighborhood."

"We can give him to someone who lives in a dog neighborhood," Mr. Davis suggested.

"Give Pete away?" wailed the twins.

"After the trouble it was to raise him," their father

remarked, "I for one would like him to live long enough to have to feed a family of his own."

"He would always be in danger here," Mrs. Davis persisted. "What about Dr. Plant? His two Scottie dogs keep cats away from his garden."

"He has lots of bird houses and feeding stands," said Dean. "He makes them with his jigsaw."

"We could go over often to see him," said Delia. "I could watch the gold fish in the pool, too."

"But we couldn't take Weej," objected Dean.

"I don't think Weejee will mind," Mr. Davis chuckled. "I believe he's beginning to wonder what he ever saw in Pete in the first place."

"All right," the twins agreed. "Let's take him to the doctor's."

"Not seeing him will be lots better than having that old Pirate cat get him," Delia added.

Mr. Davis went into the house and called Dr. Plant on the telephone. The doctor thought a pet robin in his garden would be delightful.

56

On Sunday afternoon, the Davis family cov-
ered Pete up in his basket, and walked over with

him to Dr. Plant's. They took along a few worms
for the doctor to feed Pete, to make their pet feel
at home in a strange place.

The garden was beautiful. Roses bloomed
around the marble bird bath. Water lilies were in
the pool. There were bird houses everywhere.

The doctor put Pete on his shoulder and went
over to a bird feeding stand. He took a worm

from Delia and held it up. Pete opened his mouth and waited for the doctor to feed him. The doctor laughed.

"He can do it himself when he wants to," Delia told him.

Then Dr. Plant took Pete over to the bird bath. Pete waded in and began drinking.

"Now he feels at home," said the doctor. "He has had something to eat and drink. That reminds me."

He went into the house and brought out a pitcher of cold lemonade and some brownies.

They all sat under the grape arbor and told the doctor Pete's story, right from the beginning. After a while, Delia looked around.

"Where's Pete?" she cried.

"Oh, I hope he hasn't flown away," Dr. Plant said, "before he's had a chance to get used to his new home."

"Call him," Mr. Davis said. "He's not far away."

"Here, Pete, Pete, Pete!" Dean coaxed.

Out of a tree flew the fat little bird. The doctor was bald, and his head shone brightly in the sun. Now Pete had never learned to land gently on a head. He just zoomed down and slid through the hair until he stopped.

The family stood breathless. They knew what was going to happen.

Sock! Pete landed with a thud. He slid across the doctor's shiny skull, scrabbling for a hold. Not a hair was there to stop him. He shot off into space and dropped on the soft grass. It was hard to say which was more surprised, the doctor or the robin.

It was not polite, but the Davis family doubled up with laughter.

"Does he do that often?" Dr. Plant asked, rubbing his head.

"Always," said Mrs. Davis, as soon as she could speak. "We forgot to tell you."

"I guess I'll have to wear a hat." The doctor began to laugh, too.

So they left Pete with Dr. Plant, but they went often to see their pet.

The doctor told them that every morning, when he called, Pete flew down out of the trees. But now, because the doctor wore a hat, Pete landed on his shoulder instead of his head. Pete liked the new breakfast of birdseed and chopped-up raisins that the doctor had for him. As soon as he gobbled it up, he flew back up into the trees. Whenever the doctor walked in the garden, Pete came down to keep him company.

One day, late in the summer, Pete disappeared. Dr. Plant called the Davis home.

"He may have flown back to you," he told them, "so keep a lookout."

The twins watched and watched, but Pete did not come back.

"Don't worry about it," their mother told them cheerfully. "Think how much happier Pete is with other grown-up robins. He's not a baby any more."

61

About a month later, when the days were shorter and frosty around the edges, the twins were picking the last of the green tomatoes.

"We'll wrap them in tissue paper and lay them on the attic floor," Mrs. Davis said, as she turned to go back into the house. "Sometimes they get nice and ripe that way. If we're lucky, we'll have tomato salad with our Christmas dinner."

The twins were placing the tomatoes carefully in the old basket that had once belonged to Pete. Weejee was stretched out on the hard ground of the garden path, enjoying the warmth in the fall sunshine.

Just then a bird flew low around their heads and the twins looked up. It was a robin!

"It's Pete! It's Pete!" Delia cried, pointing to the robin, now sitting on a branch of the cherry tree.

"It couldn't be," Dean said. "It doesn't look a bit like him."

"It is so Pete," Delia declared. "Here, Pete! Here,

Pete!" she called to him. "Here, Pete! Here, Pete!"

Down the robin came. He circled their heads several times, then swooped over Weejee. At this, Dean, too, was sure he was Pete.

"Mother, Mother!" the twins called. "Come out and see Pete."

Mrs. Davis came out and looked up at the bird. He sat on the porch roof just over the window where his basket had been, a sleek handsome robin.

"I believe it is Pete," she said. "He has the same white streak on his tail. Here, Pete!"

Down he came again, circled low around them, and then on strong wings soared up to the tops of the trees.

"Look at him fly!" Dean exclaimed. "It was Pete, wasn't it, Mother?"

"I'm sure it was, dear. He must have come to say good-by before he goes South for the winter. But robins almost always return to the same place after the cold weather is over," she added, "so we'll see him again in the spring, I'm sure."

"Good-by, Pete, good-by," the twins called, waving. "Come back next year!"

They felt very proud of their beautiful grown-up bird as they stood and watched him sail high over the treetops and disappear in the distance.

64